THE MIDWIFE'S APPRENTICE

by
Karen Cushman

Student Packet

Written by
Phyllis Green

Contains masters for:

1	Pre-reading Activity
5	Vocabulary Activities
1	Study Guide (three pages)
1	Comparison and Contrast Activity
3	Research Activities
5	Literary Elements Activities
2	Writing Activities
1	Comprehension Activity
1	Language Study Activity
2	Comprehension Quizzes
1	Final Examination (five sections)

PLUS

Detailed Answer Key
Rubric for Essay Writing and Grading

Note

The Clarion Books hardback edition of the book, published by Houston Mifflin, was used to prepare this guide. The page references may differ in other editions of the book.

Name _____

Preparing to Read

Directions: Look for hints about the book. Hints prepare our minds for the reading, set up our expectations, and get us ready for reading.

Sources of Hints about Books	Information Provided
Dedication	
Title	
Cover	
Teasers on the book cover or in the book jacket	
Recommendations of friends	
Recommendations of experts: book reviews and awards	

Name _____

Study Guide

Directions: These questions are to help you note the details and important themes in the book as well as the writer's craft in creating the book. Your teacher will direct you in recording answers—mentally, in written notes ready for oral discussion, or more formally. Some students find it helpful to review the questions before reading a chapter.

Chapter 1 "The Dung Heap"—Pages 1-5
1. What is the setting of the book?
2. What is a dung heap?
3. Who is Beetle?
4. How does Beetle get away from the village boys?

Chapter 2 "The Cat"—Pages 6-10
1. From what point of view is the story told?
2. How does the author get you interested in the story?
3. Why doesn't Beetle give the cat more of a name?
4. What happens to the cat at the hands of the village boys?

Chapter 3 "The Midwife"—Pages 11-16
1. Identify the midwife with at least three names or descriptions.
2. What does the midwife charge for her services?
3. What supplies does the midwife carry in her basket?
4. Describe Beetle's life in the midwife's cottage.

Chapter 4 "The Miller's Wife"—Pages 17-24
1. What is the secret revealed in the chapter?
2. What are the circumstances that bring Beetle to the miller's house?
3. Why does the midwife slap the miller's wife?
4. Why is Beetle called "Brainless Brat," "Clodpole," and "Good-for-Nothing"?

Chapter 5 "The Merchant"—Pages 25-32
1. How does Beetle meet a merchant?
2. What gift does Beetle receive at the fair?
3. Who is Alyce?

Chapter 6 "The Naming"—Pages 33-39
1. What names does Beetle suggest for the cat?
2. How does Beetle come to be addressed as Alyce?

Chapter 7 "The Devil"—Pages 40-47
1. Why do the villagers begin to think of witches and devils?
2. How does Alyce play on the villager's concerns with witches and devils?

Chapter 8 "The Twins"—Pages 48-53
1. How do Alyce and the cat enjoy picking up apples?
2. How do Alyce and Will calm Tansy?
3. Why is Alyce gaining more respect from the villagers?

Chapter 9 "The Bailiff's Wife's Baby"—Pages 54-60
1. How has Alyce changed since the midwife found her in the dung pile?
2. How does Alyce deal with the village boys' teasing of the cat?
3. How does she deal with the birth of Alyce Little?

Chapter 10 "The Boy"—Pages 61-66
1. Who is the boy in the chapter's title?
2. How is Alyce taking charge of her education?

Chapter 11 "The Leaving"—Pages 67-71
1. How differently do Alyce and the midwife react to Matthew Blunt's request for Alyce to help his mother deliver another baby?
2. Why is the chapter titled "The Leaving"?

Chapter 12 "The Inn"—Pages 72-81
1. What is the setting for Chapter 12?
2. What is unique about this setting?
3. How does Alyce's education continue in this chapter?
4. What is an encyclopedic compendium?

Chapter 13 "Visitors"—Pages 82-88
1. What kind of an innkeeper is Jennet?
2. How is Alyce adjusting to life at the inn?
3. Why are the spring visitors at the inn of particular interest to Alyce?
4. What is the difference between giving up and failure? How is this difference relevant to the story?

Chapter 14 "The Manor"—Pages 89-94
1. How do Girtle and Rosebud cause Alyce to take action?
2. Who does Alyce meet in her manor visit?
3. Who gives Alyce information about Edward? What is this information?

Chapter 15 "Edward"—Pages 95-103
1. Why is this a joyful chapter?
2. Identify the following: greasy yellow soap, a man's job, Lord Arnulf, differences between what one imagines and what is.

Chapter 16 "The Baby"—Pages 104-111
1. Who is the baby in chapter 16?
2. How do the events in chapter 16 change Alyce?

Chapter 17 "The Midwife's Apprentice"—Pages 112-117
1. How is this chapter a turning point in the book?
2. What is the mood at the end of the book?

Author's Note—Pages 118-122
1. How is the author's note helpful to you?
2. What is the topic of the author's note?

Things to Identify

Directions: Identify these items mentioned in the book. Include your information source.

Item	Definition and Details	Source
dung beetle		
wimple		
borage leaves		
comfrey tonic		
rebec		
gittern		
sackbut		

Name _____

Put Yourself in the Picture: Identification

Directions: Choose two of the items below to investigate and identify for a class bulletin board or book. Be sure to include your sources.

Magna Carta	Lady Day	Spanish Armada
Saint Cuthbert	The Crusades	Saint Swithin's Day
Feudalism	All Hallow's Eve	Walpurgis Night
Martinmas		

the information:

the sources:

the information:

the sources:

Investigating Medieval

Directions: Get a handle on the setting of the book.

- What does the word medieval mean? _____

  _____

  _____

  _____

  _____

- What images are most prominent in medieval scenes? _____

  _____

  _____

  _____

  _____

- What other words or terms are related to medieval? _____

  _____

  _____

  _____

  _____

- What was happening in Medieval England? _____

  _____

  _____

  _____

  _____

 Comparing the Middle Ages and Contemporary Times

Directions: Fill in the chart to indicate various aspects of human life in the two periods.

Situation	Middle Ages	Contemporary Times
medical treatment		
pest control		
dental care		
means of communication		
forms of entertainment		

Vocabulary Words—Chapters 1-6

Directions: Look over these words prior to reading each chapter. Underline or highlight those words you don't know. Either figure them out from the context of the story, or look them up in a dictionary.

Chapter 1
moiling
stench
reeked
mucking
bailiff

Chapter 2
taunting
bedeviled

Chapter 3
curdled
wimple
borage
ragwort
columbine
stanching
bryony
wooly nightshade
jasper stone
elder leaves
clodpole
whiffler
feverfew
haggling
midwifery
comfrey

Chapter 4
milkwort
wormwood
comfrey
nettle
exertions

Chapter 5
replenish
score
boneset
abbey
meandered
soothsayers
quivered
forenoon
solemnity

Chapter 6
purslane
lentil
daft
dartmoor
lardy
columbine
cuttlefish
clotweed
shrovetide
wimble
pluck

Vocabulary Words—Chapters 7-12

Directions: Look over the words prior to reading each chapter. Underline or highlight the words you don't know. Either figure them out from the context of the book, or look them up in a dictionary.

Chapter 7
fared
magpie
dewclaws
paternosters
gluttony

Chapter 8
casks
fermenting

Chapter 9
writhing
mewling
betook

Chapter 10
mallows
corpus
threshing
tunic

Chapter 11
quivered
tumult
privies
Martinmas

Chapter 12
exertions
faraway
humors
chickadees
teemed
rebecs
gitterns
sackbuts
mucking
blight
renowned
compendium
ampleness
tantalizing
compliant

Name _____

Vocabulary Words—Chapters 13-17

Directions: Look over the words prior to reading the chapter. Underline or highlight those words you don't know. Either figure them out from the context of the story, or look them up in a dictionary.

Chapter 13
overyeast
mutton
sorrel
swig

Chapter 14
hedgeroses
suckle
desolate

Chapter 15
tweaked
bleating
bawling
lathering
mayhap

Chapter 16
compassion
innards
lout

Chapter 17
larkspur
whorls
surfeit

Author's Note
innovation
disrepute

Vocabulary—Multiple Meanings

Directions: Look at the word families below. Each unique spelling has several meanings. Choose two of the meanings and write appropriate sentences for them.

SCORE: notch to keep tally; evaluative record; group items; written musical composition for orchestra or vocal; a debt

ADDRESS: to make a formal speech; to mark a destination, as address a letter; to adjust and aim the club, as address the ball in golf; number assigned to a location

HOT: possessing great heat; being at a high temperature; highly spiced; radioactive; explosive; recently stolen; fast; new, fresh, as hot off the press; good or impressive; ridiculous or incredible; angry; in trouble, as being in hot water

FLOUR: a soft, fine powdery substance; to cover or coat with flour; to make into flour

SWEET: having a sugary taste; containing or derived from sugar; pleasing to the senses; gratifying; lovable; fresh; not spoiled; free of acid; performing jazz in this way; a dear person; anything relatively sweet served as a dessert (British)

STORES: shops; supplies; warehouse

DEAR: loved; highly regarded; high-priced

HUMOR: funniness; one of four fluids in the body; mood

© Novel Units, Inc.

14

Synonym Chains

Directions: Choose five words from the book to use to start synonym chains. For example:

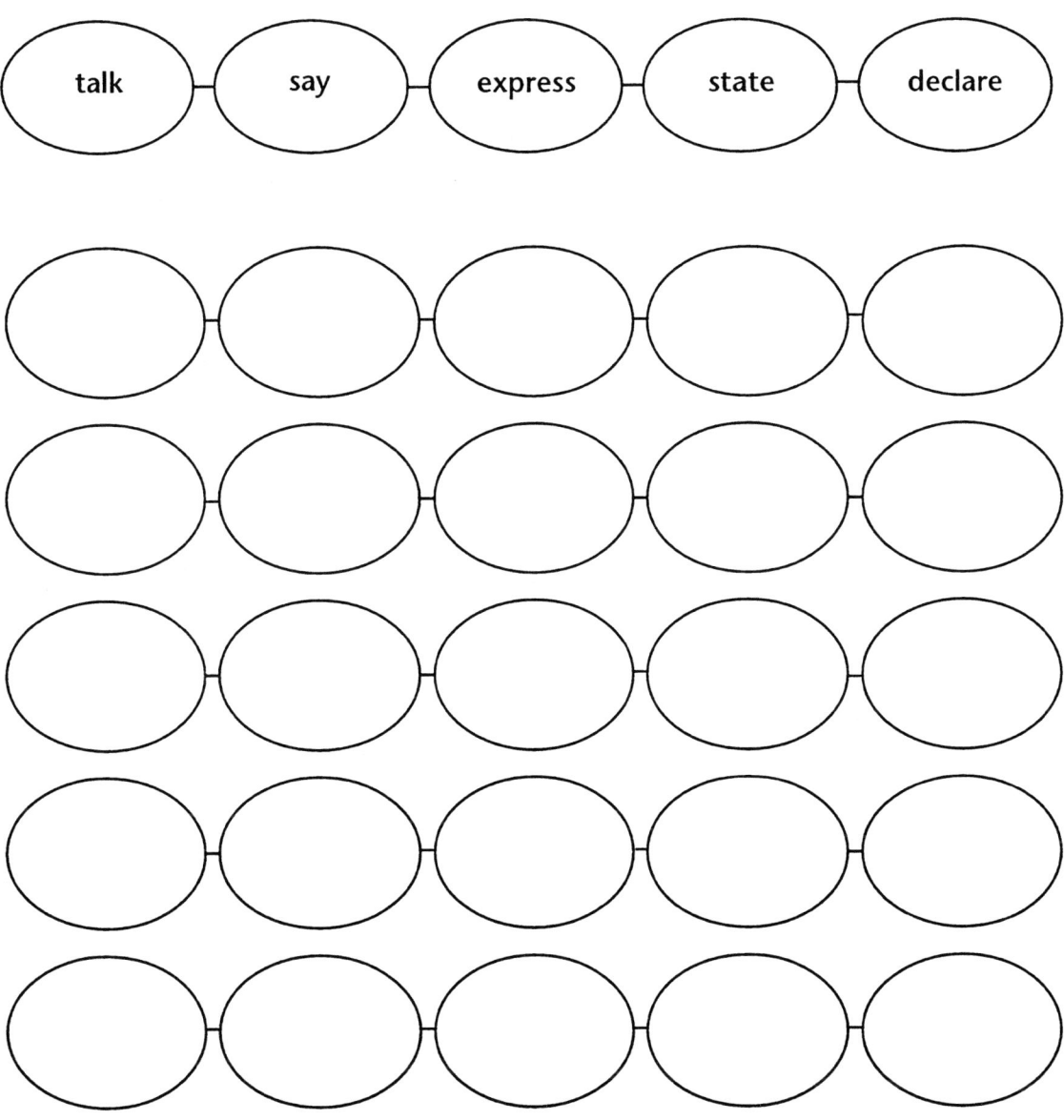

Name _____

Comparison

The Setting of the Book and the Place Where You Live

Directions: Record what you know of the book's setting with page references. Then make a comparison to the place where you live.

Comparison

A setting in the book (and page #)	The place where you live

The Author's Style

Directions: An author's style is his or her way of writing. Choose three short chapters to read carefully for the writer's style.

How long are the sentences? (average number of words)	What kind of words does the author use?	Are there any similes or metaphors?
How many sentences are there in a paragraph?	How do you feel after reading a chapter? What is the mood?	Are there any flashbacks or foreshadowings?
What kind of names are used?	What kind of chapter titles are used?	What is the author's point of view?

Write one sentence to summarize the author's style: _____

_____

Character Cluster

Directions: Record information about the book's characters in the boxes provided.

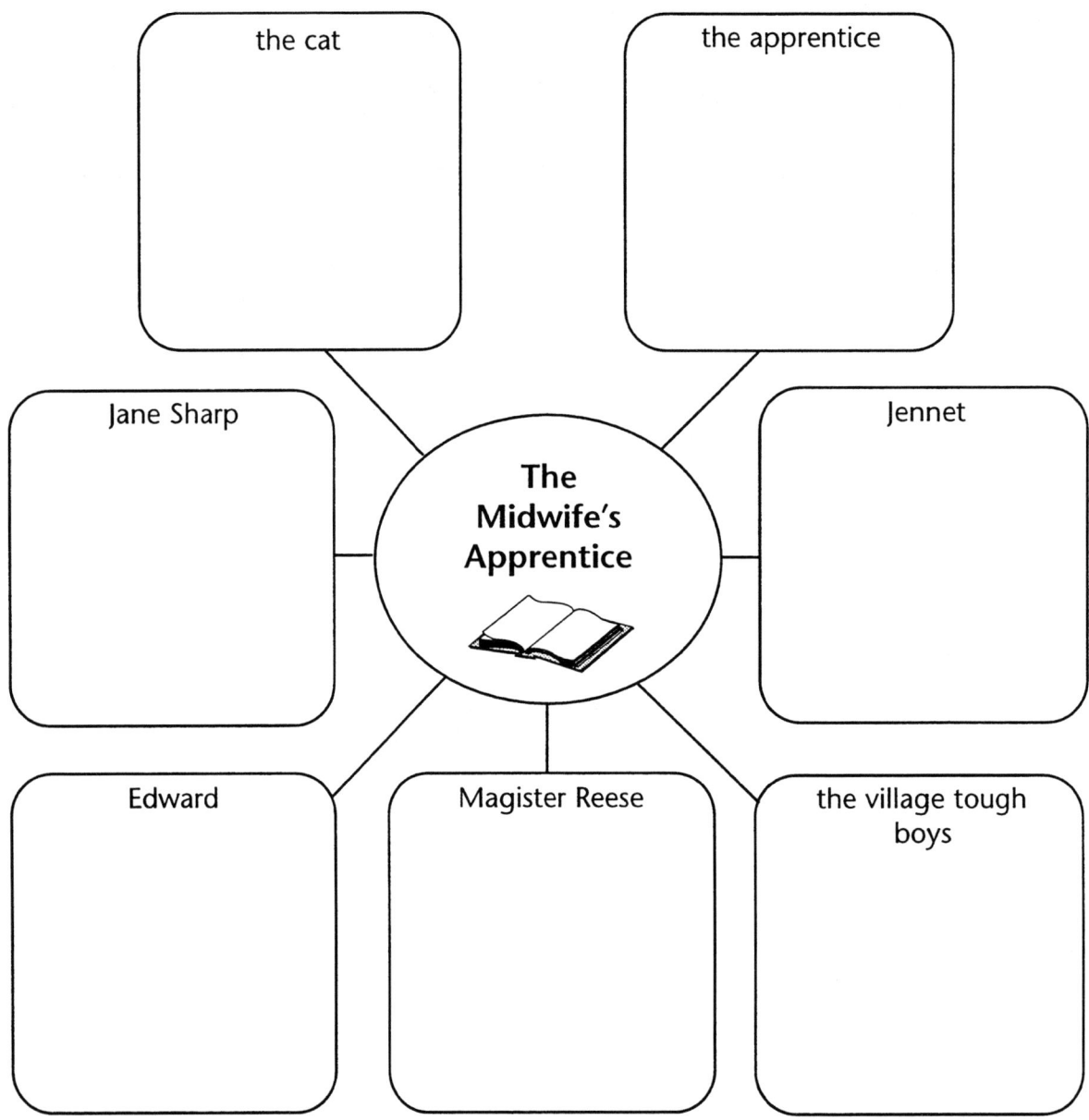

the cat

the apprentice

Jane Sharp

The Midwife's Apprentice

Jennet

Edward

Magister Reese

the village tough boys

Writing in Similes

Directions: Consider these scenes and people from the book. Describe each in a simile. Choose a comparison to someone or something in your world and experience.

The midwife Jane Sharp _____

_____

_____

Beetle_____

_____

_____

the cat _____

_____

_____

the midwife's cottage_____

_____

_____

Saint Swithin's Day Fair_____

_____

_____

What's in a Name?

Directions: Collect the most interesting names you've found in books you've read. Then choose one of the writing prompts for a short paragraph.

Names from my reading:

- My choice for the best-named character from a book is_____.
- Authors find names in odd places.
- Beetle is right; this business of having a name was harder than it seemed.
- I especially like or dislike my own name because...

Cause and Effect

Directions: Listed below are parts of cause-and-effect relationships from chapters one through ten of *The Midwife's Apprentice*. Fill in the missing part for each relationship.

1. **Cause:** The town boys were bored and into mischief. They saw a cat nearby.

   Effect: _____

   _____

2. **Cause:** _____

   _____

   Effect: Beetle decided to call herself Alyce.

3. **Cause:** The midwife and the baker were meeting and kissing and hugging.

   Effect: _____

   _____

4. **Cause:** _____

   _____

   Effect: Alyce grew in esteem among the villagers.

5. **Cause:** _____

   _____

   Effect: Alyce names Edward.

Name _____

Writing Circle

Directions: Choose a space from each of the three circles below—a character, a situation, and something to include. Then write a story using the three elements.

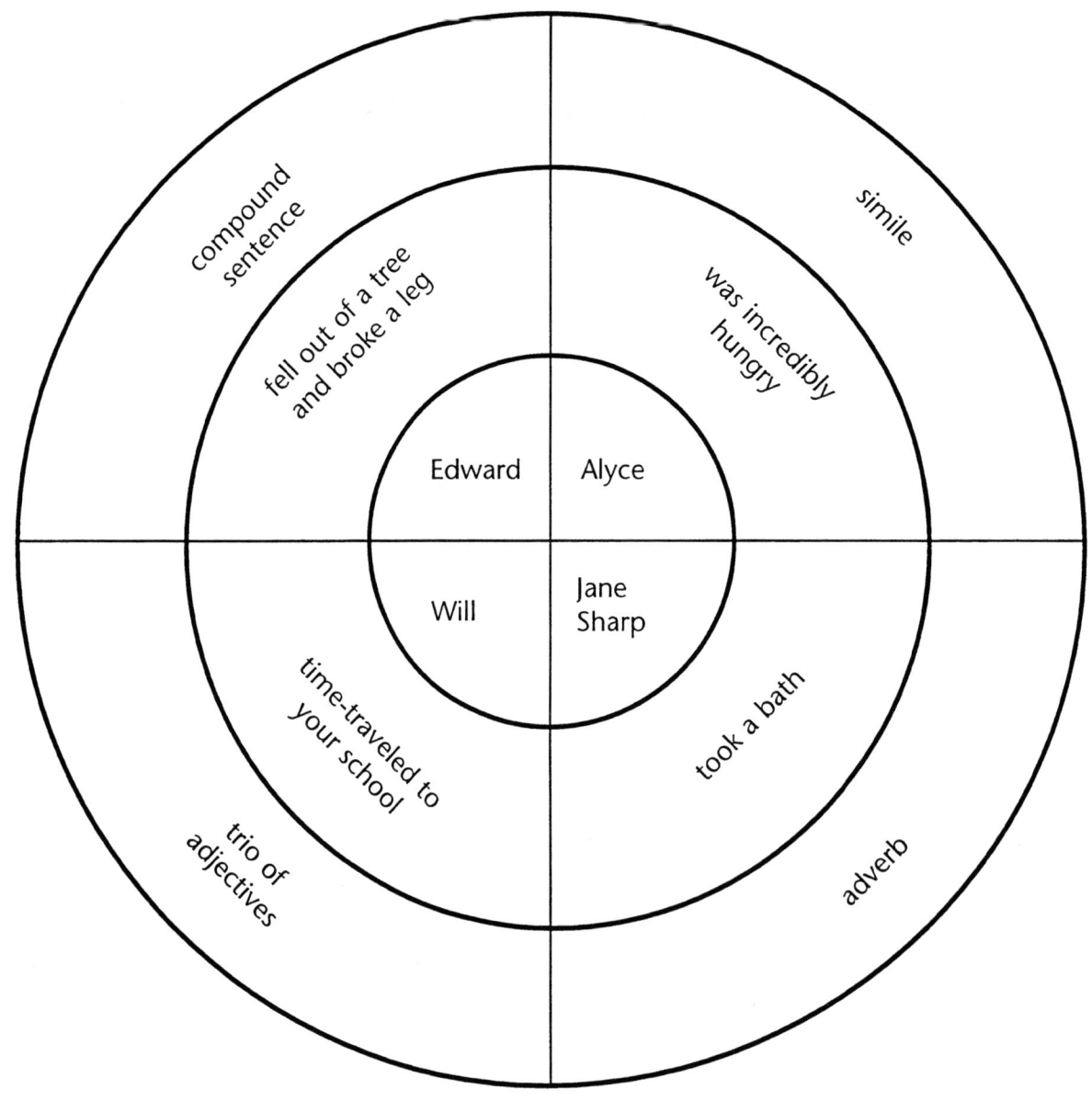

Name _____

Story Pyramid

Directions: Review the plot of the story by completing the story pyramid.

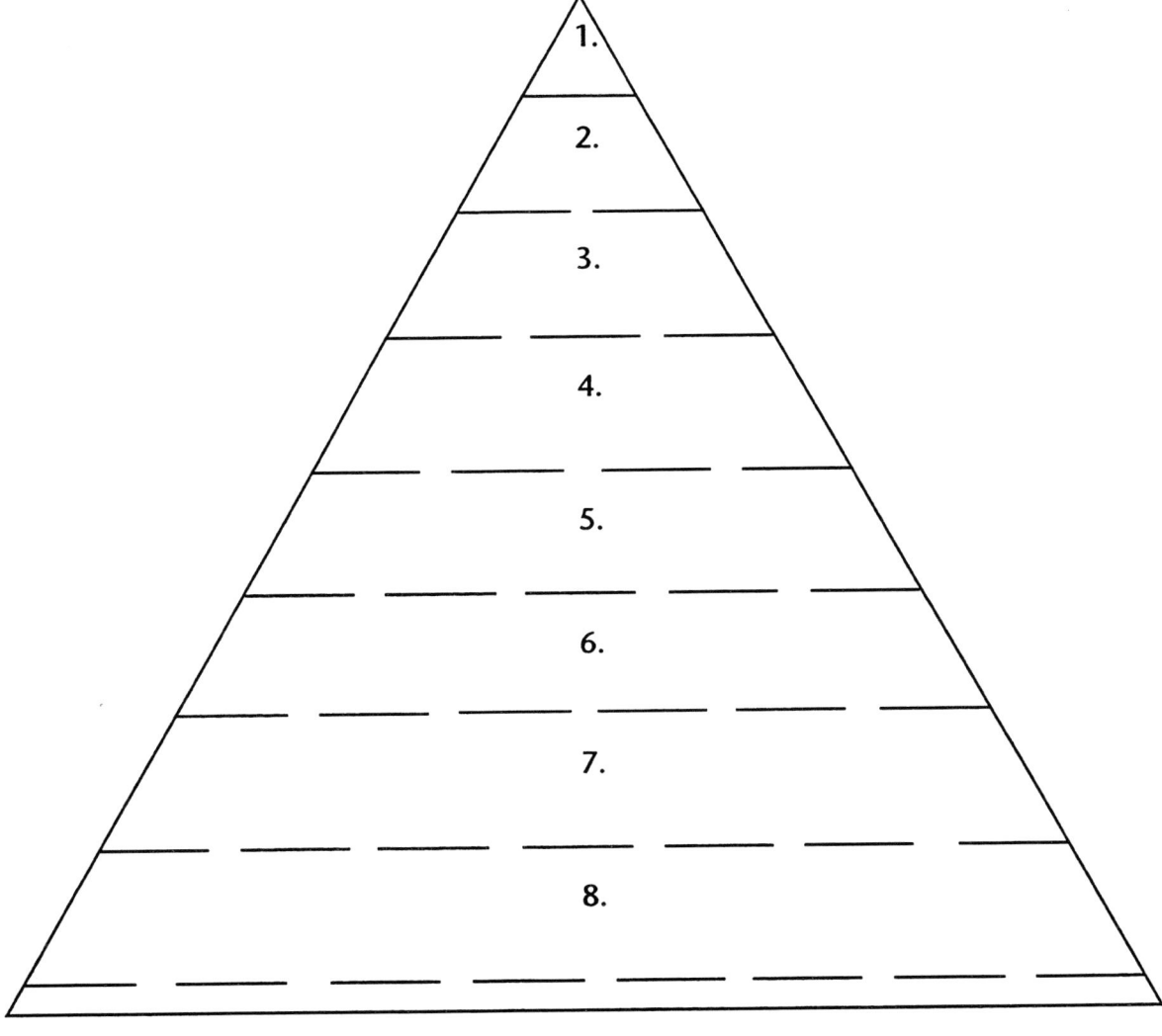

1. One word naming the main character.
2. Two words describing the main character.
3. Three words describing the setting.
4. Four words describing the problem.
5. Five words that represent the first main event.
6. Six words that represent the second main event.
7. Seven words for the third main event.
8. Eight words for the resolution of the story.

Bio-Poem

Directions: Create a Bio-Poem for the midwife's apprentice.

- Line 1: First name only
- Line 2: Four traits that describe that person
- Line 3: Sibling of...(or son/daughter of...)
- Line 4: Lover of...(three people or ideas)
- Line 5: Who feels...(three items)
- Line 6: Who fears...(three items)
- Line 7: Who would like to see...(three items)
- Line 8: Resident of...(city, state, street, etc.)
- Line 9: Last name only

1 _____**Beetle**_____

2 _____

3 _____

4 _____

5 _____

6 _____

7 _____

8 _____

9 _____**Alyce**_____

Name _____

Quiz # 1—Chapters 1-6

Directions: Choose the best answer, a, b, or c, to complete each statement.

1. The main character in the book is a) unwashed and unnourished, b) a lady-in-waiting, c) a mangy dog.

2. Beetle a) befriends the midwife's cat, b) rescues the cat from a bag and eel, c) hates cats and dogs because they pester her.

3. The midwife a) is married to the miller, b) births children because of her own experience with her twelve children, c) has a sharp nose.

4. Most of the book's chapters a) are long, b) have titles starting with "the," c) have at least one illustration.

5. Karen Cushman a) wrote the book, b) reviewed the book, c) had no relationship with the book.

6. The miller's wife a) is a sweet caring mother, b) helps her husband at the mill, c) cries that she no longer wants the child.

7. Saint Swithin's Day Fair a) is a joy to Beetle, b) is rained out, c) is a church festival.

8. Beetle chooses a name because a) she hates the name Beetle, b) the midwife dislikes the name Beetle, c) she is mistaken for someone named Alyce.

9. Alyce and Will a) fall down on a riverbank, b) hate each other, c) are long-lost siblings.

10. The midwife's apprentice a) is an old withered woman, b) can't learn the midwifery craft, c) finds her life and lot improved in the midwife's cottage.

Name _____

Quiz # 2—Chapters 7-12

Directions: Choose the best answer, a, b, or c, to complete each statement.

1. Alyce takes revenge on those who harmed her by a) putting a hex on them, b) leading the villagers to their evil with fake devil footsteps, c) poisoning their food.

2. Alyce helps Tansy by a) fetching apples to make cider for her, b) singing to calm her, c) sending the cat to her.

3. A good nut year means a) a good baby year, b) a long winter, c) happy squirrels.

4. The bailiff's wife's baby a) is named Alyce Little, b) is a small boy, c) is Tansy's twin.

5. The bailiff a) pays the midwife double for aiding in his wife's delivery of their baby, b) arrests the midwife for robbery, c) dismisses Jane because the apprentice had delivered their baby.

6. Alyce learned midwifery a) from an ancient book, b) by secretly watching Jane Sharp, c) at the inn.

7. Alyce leaves the midwife's cottage because a) it smells to terrible, b) she failed Emma in delivering her baby, c) Jane Sharp was just too sharp.

8. The letter Z a) was too hard for Alyce to learn, b) seemed mean, c) was the most beautiful letter.

9. Alyce wishes for a) a yellow ribbon for her hair, b) the ability to read, c) a place in this world.

10. The book is set in a) contemporary times, b) the middle ages, c) 1900.

Name _____

Final Examination—The Midwife's Apprentice

Part 1
Directions: Match the numbers with appropriate lettered responses. There are extra lettered items.

Words	Responses
_____ 1. abbey	a. sheriff's assistant
_____ 2. bailiff	b. submissive
_____ 3. curdled	c. forlorn
_____ 4. compendium	d. excessive eating or drinking
_____ 5. compliant	e. something new
_____ 6. surfeit	f. internal organs
_____ 7. desolate	g. feed to fullness or excess
_____ 8. innovation	h. confident
_____ 9. innards	i. monastery
_____ 10. gluttony	j. coagulated
	k. prince
	l. castle
	m. short, complete summary

Part 2
Directions: Use **two** of the following words in a sentence: *wimple, midwifery, innovation, larkspur, clotweed, shrovetide, nettle, soothsayers.* Be sure your sentences reveal that you understand the meaning of the words.

_____

_____

_____

_____

_____

_____

_____

Part 3

Directions: Choose the best response (a, b, or c) to complete the following statements:

1. The midwife's apprentice a) is found in a dung heap by Jane Sharp, b) marries the crown prince, c) raises cats for sale.

2. The midwife's apprentice a) is named Alyce for her mother, b) lives in a cave on the edge of town, c) is homeless.

3. Jane Sharp a) is warm and compassionate in her dealings with her clients, b) was training in midwifery at the abbey, c) is harsh and sharp in her manner.

4. Edward a) is the king's cousin, b) stays at the inn while writing his book, c) is befriended by Alyce.

5. Alyce's wish in life is a) a full belly, a contented heart and a place in the world, b) a name, c) a family for whom she can care.

6. The author would consider the medieval period a) filled with knights, castles and battles, b) a hard time for common people, c) dominated by the church.

7. Magister Reese a) is harsh and crude, b) has regal manners and pretensions, c) befriends Alyce.

8. Alyce comes to cleanliness a) because the midwife demands it, b) accidentally when she helps with the sheep shearing, c) because she plans to join Magister Reese on his travels.

9. Will Russett a) pushes Alyce into the dung heap, b) winks at Alyce when he sees her at the inn, c) helps Edward find a place to stay.

10. The midwife would choose as a maxim for life, a) "service over self," b) "keep trying; don't give up," c) "you catch more bees with honey."

Part 4

Directions: Match the numbers with appropriate lettered responses. There are extra lettered items.

_____ 1. Alyce		a.	Alyce's stray cat
_____ 2. bailiff		b.	"cheats" customers
_____ 3. Beetle		c.	blind
_____ 4. Edward		d.	recommends Alyce to her sister
_____ 5. Will Russet		e.	the midwife's apprentice
_____ 6. Jane Sharp		f.	his wife is assisted in delivery by Alyce
_____ 7. the miller's wife		g.	abbot
_____ 8. Tansy		h.	visits Alyce at the inn
_____ 9. Jennet		i.	homeless boy
_____ 10. John Dark		j.	sharp tongued with a difficult birth
		k.	mother of twins
		l.	given a lot of bread
		m.	the reader

Extra Credit: Choose two characters to describe and compare.

_____

_____

_____

_____

_____

_____

_____

© Novel Units, Inc.

29

Part 5—Writing

Directions: Choose one of the following questions to answer in two or three short paragraphs. Be sure to refer to the book and give reasons for your answers.

A. The Middle Ages is a period in which I'd love to have lived.

B. If I were casting the book as a TV movie, I'd choose_____ to play the midwife's apprentice.

C. Karen Cushman has a promising future as a novelist.

D. Alyce will grow and mature into_____.

_____

_____

_____

_____

_____

_____

_____

_____

_____

_____

_____

_____

Answer Key

Study Guide

Chapter 1: 1. The story takes place in fourteenth century England. 2. It is a pile of manure. 3. She is a homeless girl who sleeps in the dung heap to keep warm. 4. The midwife happens by and scares off the boys. **Chapter 2:** 1. The story is told in third person from Beetle's point of view. 2. She introduces Beetle and an unfamiliar setting. 3. Beetle doesn't have a name so she treats the animal in the same transitory way she has been treated herself. 4. The boys put the cat in a bag with an eel and throw both into the river, testing whether the cat can best the eel. **Chapter 3:** 1. Jane Sharp, the only midwife in the village, is energetic about her job, but not joyful. (page 11) 2. Payment is a silver penny, a length of newly woven cloth, the best layer in the hen house, or whatever the midwife negotiated. 3. She carries various herbs and clean linen. (page 13) 4. She receives two meals a day. In the morning she does household chores and in the afternoon she and the cat go to the woods. She accompanies the midwife on her birthing visits. **Chapter 4:** 1. The midwife and the baker are kissing. 2. The midwife is absent with the baker. Beetle is admonished not to reveal the location, so Beetle is dragged to the miller's cottage to help with a birth. 3. She slaps the miller's wife to get the miller's wife out of her hysteria. 4. The midwife deals in insults and Beetle is unable to help the miller's wife. **Chapter 5:** 1. The midwife's ankle injury makes it impossible for her to go to the fair. She sends Beetle instead. 2. Beetle receives a comb with the image of a sleeping cat carved on it. 3. She is a mysterious person who can read, for whom Beetle is mistaken. **Chapter 6:** 1. Names Beetle suggests for the cat are Willow, Purslane, Gypsy Moth, Lentil, Earth Pine, Dartmoor, Cheesemaker, Holly, Pork, Columbine, Cuttlefish, Clotweed, Shrovetide, Wimble, and Purr. (pages 34-35) 2. Beetle decides to call herself Alyce after the mysterious reader. **Chapter 7:** 1. They are superstitious and some odd things had happened. (page 41) 2. She uses blocks of wood carved in the shape of the hooves of some unknown beast to lead villagers to those who taunted and tormented her. The villagers catch her tormentors in wrongdoing. **Chapter 8:** 1. Alyce tastes the different varieties of apples and the cat imagines ears and tails on the apples and chases them. 2. Alyce sings to her and rubs her. Will works to move the calves. 3. She helps birthing the twin calves, a lucky omen. She grows in knowledge and skills. **Chapter 9:** 1. She is more capable and assertive. Others treat her better. 2. She calls off the boys with threats that she has a bottle of "rats blood and viper's flesh" which will change them into women. 3. When the midwife leaves to attend Lady Agnes' delivery of her first son, Beetle calms Joan, and Little Alyce is born feet first. **Chapter 10:** 1. Edward is a homeless waif that Alyce befriends. 2. She watches while the midwife works. **Chapter 11:** 1. Alice is surprised and the midwife is furious at Alyce for stealing her mothers. 2. At the end of the chapter Alyce runs away from the midwife's cottage. **Chapter 12:** 1. The setting of Chapter 12 is John Dark's inn. 2. John Dark's inn is a modest place, really a large stone cottage with a room over a big kitchen, a loft above the stable, and tables in the hall for sleeping on or under. 3. She learns letters from Magister Richard Reese. 4. Richard Reese's book **Chapter 13:** 1. She is profitable, willing to take economies. 2. Jennet is well-content with her work. Alyce is a quick study, learning with little direct instruction. 3. The carpenter's assistant, Will Russet, and the midwife are spring visitors at the inn. 4. Giving up means not sticking with a task that seems difficult. Failure is an inability to do a task. Alyce isn't a failure in midwifery; she just gives up when a birth is slow and hard. **Chapter 14:** 1. She sees the love between the cow and her calf and thinks of Edward, who showed love to her. 2. Alyce meets men sharpening hoes and sickles, a kitchen maid, a blacksmith and apprentices. 3. A cook tells her that Edward, who is helping in the kitchen, talks of his sister Alyce. **Chapter 15:** 1. It tells of the reunion of Alyce and Edward. 2. Identifications are as follows: greasy yellow soap is used to wash sheep; a man's job is helping with washing the sheep; Lord Arnulf is Lord of the Manor; it is the difference between what one imagines or fantasizes,

---

versus reality. **Chapter 16:** 1. The baby is the merchant's wife's baby boy. 2. She gains confidence in herself; she laughs. **Chapter 17:** 1. Alyce decides to leave the inn and return to the midwife. 2. The ending is upbeat and hopeful. **Author's Note:** 1. The note gives information about midwifery and puts the topic into a contemporary context. 2. The topic of the author's note is midwifery.

Cause and Effect Activity
1. Effect: The boys threw the cat and an eel into a bag to see who would survive. **2. Cause:** At the fair, someone called Beetle Alyce, mistaking her for someone else who could read. **3. Effect:** There was a lot of bread at the midwife's cottage and the midwife seemed to be absent a lot.
4. Cause: Alyce helps to deliver Tansy's twins. **5. Cause:** Edward is homeless and asks for the King's name to take as his own.
Quiz # 1: 1. a 2. b 3. c 4. b 5. a 6. c 7. a 8. c 9. a 10. c
Quiz #2: 1. b 2. b 3. a 4. a 5. c 6. b 7. b 8. b 9. c 10. b

Final Examination
Part 1: 1. i 2. a 3. j 4. m 5. b 6. g 7. c 8. e 9. f 10. d
Part 2:

wimple:	cloth wound around the head and drawn into folds beneath the chin, so that it frames the face
midwifery:	profession of assisting in childbirth by another woman
innovation:	something new
larkspur:	plant of genus, phinium
clotweed:	xanthium strumarium; rare weeds
nettle:	plant of genus, urtica; plants that have toothed leaves covered with hairs that secrete a stinging fluid that affects the skin on contact.
soothsayer:	prophet who claims to foretell events

Part 3: 1. a 2. c 3. c 4. c 5. a 6. b 7. c 8. b 9. b 10. b
Part 4: 1. m 2. f 3. e 4. i 5. h 6. l 7. j 8. k 9. b 10. c